love all creatures

The Islamic Foundation

Reprinted 1982, 1985, 1990 (revised edition)

ISBN 0 86037 077 1

MUSLIM CHILDREN'S LIBRARY

General Editors:
Khurram Murad and Arshad Gamiet

LOVE ALL CREATURES

Writer and researcher:
M.S. Kayani

Editorial: Mrs. B.R. Lewis
Designer: Jerzy Karo

These stories are about the Prophet and his Companions and, though woven around authentic ahadith, should be regarded only as stories.

Published by:
The Islamic Foundation
Markfield Dawah Centre,
Ratby Lane, Markfield,
Leicester, LE6 0RN, UK.

Quran House, P.O. Box 30611,
Nairobi, Kenya

P.M.B. 3193, Kano, Nigeria

British Library Cataloguing in Publication Data
Kayani, M S
Love all creatures. —
(Muslim children's library).
1. Muhammad, *Prophet* — Juvenile literature
I. Title   II. Series
297' 63 BP75
ISBN 0 86037 0771

Printed by:
Joseph Ball (Printers) Ltd,
Leicester

MUSLIM CHILDREN'S LIBRARY

An Introduction.

Here is a new series of books, but with a difference, for children of all ages. Published by the Islamic Foundation, the Muslim Children's Library has been produced to provide young people with something they cannot perhaps find anywhere else.

Most of today's children's books aim only to entertain and inform or to teach some necessary skills, but not to develop the inner and moral resources. Entertainment and skills by themselves impart nothing of value to life unless a child is also helped to discover deeper meaning in himself and the world around him. Yet there is no place in them for God, who alone gives meaning to life and the universe, nor for the divine guidance brought by His prophets, following which can alone ensure an integrated development of the total personality.

Such books, in fact, rob young people of access to true knowledge. They give them no unchanging standards of right and wrong, nor any incentives to live by what is right and refrain from what is wrong. The result is that all too often the young enter adult life in a state of social alienation, bewilderment, unable to cope with the seemingly unlimited choices of the world around them. The situation is especially devastating for the Muslim child as he may grow up cut off from his culture and values.

The Muslim Children's Library aspires to remedy this deficiency by showing children the deeper meaning of life and the world around them; by pointing them along paths leading to an integrated development of all aspects of their personality; by helping to give them the capacity to cope with the complexities of their world, both personal and social; by opening vistas into a world extending far beyond this life; and, to a Muslim child especially, by providing a fresh and strong faith, a dynamic commitment, an indelible sense of identity, a throbbing yearning and an urge to struggle, all rooted in Islam.

The books aim to help a child anchor his development on the rock of divine guidance, and to understand himself and relate to himself and others in just and meaningful ways. They relate directly to his soul and intellect, to his emotions and imagination, to his motives and desires, to his anxieties and hopes — indeed, to every aspect of his fragile, but potentially rich personality. At the same time it is recognised that for a book to hold a child's attention, he must enjoy reading it; it should therefore arouse his curiosity and entertain him as well. The style, the language, the illustrations and the production of the books are all geared to this goal. They provide moral education, but not through sermons or ethical abstractions.

Although these books are based entirely on Islamic teachings and the vast Muslim heritage, they should be of equal interest and value to all children, whatever their country or creed; for Islam is a universal religion, the natural path.

Adults, too, may find much of use in them. In particular, Muslim parents and teachers will find that they provide what they have for so long been so badly needing. The books will include texts on the Quran, the Sunnah and other basic sources and teachings of Islam, as well as history, stories and anecdotes for supplementary reading. Each book will cater for a particular age group, classified into five: pre-school, 5-8 years, 8-11, 11-14 and 14-17.

We invite parents and teachers to use these books in homes and classrooms, at breakfast tables and bedside and encourage children to derive maximum benefit from them. At the same time their greatly valued observations and suggestions are highly welcome.

To the young reader we say: you hold in your hands books which may be entirely different from those you have been reading till now, but we sincerely hope you will enjoy them; try, through these books, to understand youself, your life, your experiences and the universe around you. They will open before your eyes new paths and models in life that you will be curious to explore and find exciting and rewarding to follow. May God be with you forever.

And may He bless with His mercy and acceptance our humble contribution to the urgent and gigantic task of producing books for a new generation of people, a task which we have undertaken in all humility and hope.

Khurram Jah Murad
Director General

contents

introduction »« an act of virtue

The Prophet Muhammad (peace and blessings of Allah be upon him),* was always mindful of the small creatures and animals which live upon the earth. These small creatures are all God's creatures, and *must* be treated with kindness and care. The Blessed Prophet always taught that this was so, and that it was the duty of all Muslims to observe this rule.

'You will be rewarded by Allah for your acts of kindness towards living creatures', the Blessed Prophet said.

Allah wants men to look after animals. Plants and trees needed care and respect, too.

'Even looking after plants and trees is an act of virtue', said the Blessed Prophet.

'For a Muslim', he said, 'it is an act of charity to plant a tree or till a land where birds or people or animals come and eat of its fruits.'

May Allah bless His Prophet and shower peace upon him. He came to this world as a blessing for men and animals and all creatures that live on the earth.

The Blessed Prophet told his Companions many stories about kindness to animals. He told them how Allah rewards such kindness, but punishes cruelty. Here are some of the stories the Blessed Prophet told about some of the ways we can be kind to animals and care for them as Allah has commanded.

---

*Muslims are required to invoke Allah's blessings and peace upon the Prophet whenever his name is mentioned.

1·the little ants

The Blessed Prophet and his Companions once paused during a journey and made a camp where they could rest. The Blessed Prophet went round the camp, talking to the men, and making sure that everything was all right.

Then, not far away, he saw a fire. Someone had lit the fire to keep himself warm. The Blessed Prophet walked over towards the man who had lit the fire, to talk to him.

Suddenly, he saw that not far away, there was an ant hill. The ants could be seen running about near the hill, working very hard, as ants do. Some of the ants were further away from the ant hill than the others, and the Blessed Prophet saw that they were getting very close to the fire which the man had lit. If they came much closer, the ants might be burned up or harmed in some way.

The Blessed Prophet was very disturbed to see this. The ants were in danger. That meant that God's living creatures were in danger.

'Who has made this fire?' he asked.

The man who had made the fire looked up.

'I made the fire, O Messenger of Allah!' he replied.

'It is cold and I wanted to make myself warm.'

'Quick!' the Blessed Prophet told him. 'Put out the fire! Put out the fire!'

The man obeyed at once. He took a blanket and beat the fire until the flames died away.

Then, the man looked round and saw that there were ants near to where the fire had been. He realized then

that the Blessed Prophet had been worried about the ants. He did not want the fire to hurt them and in his great mercy he had ordered the fire to be put out.

Ever afterwards, the man would always remember to look round carefully before he made a fire.

'There might be ants or other animals nearby', he would say to himself. 'And Allah forbids that any man should hurt them!'

2 · a thirsty dog

One day, the Blessed Prophet told his Companions a story about a man who went on a journey.

The day the man left home to start on his journey, it was very hot. The sun was bright and blazing in the sky. The earth beneath the man's feet was burning hot. The man had not gone very far before his head began to ache. The heat made him feel very tired. His mouth felt dry.

'I must find some water, or I shall die of thirst', he said to himself.

He began to look for water. The first well he came to was dry, and so was the second well. The man began to feel hotter and hotter then, at last, he found another well, and saw that it was full of water.

'Allah be praised!' the man said. 'I have found water at last. Now I can drink.'

Then, the man remembered that he had not brought a rope or a bucket with him. He searched round the well and looked inside, then searched again. But there was no bucket or rope to be found.

How am I going to get the water? he thought. There was only one way. He had to climb down into the well.

Carefully the man climbed over the side of the well and began to climb downwards. He was so tired from the heat that he found it very difficult. But after a while he began to feel better because the well was cool inside.

At long last, the man reached the water. He put his hand down, and felt the cool water between his fingers. It was a wonderful feeling. He drank the water until he no longer felt thirsty. Then, he rubbed the water over his face and neck. He dipped the corners of his robe in the water so that they would keep him cool for a while when he left the well. The man felt much better now.

Water is the liquid of life, he thought. 'And Allah is the giver of water! Allah be praised!'

When the man had finished, he began to climb up out of the well. It was difficult and took a lot of strength. But at last, the man reached the top of the well and climbed out again onto the hot ground.

Suddenly, he heard a sound. It was a dog whining and crying. The man turned round and saw the dog nearby. The poor animal was very thirsty. Its mouth was open and it was panting. The dog was sniffing at the ground and the man could see that it was tired and thirsty.

The dog came up to him and began to lick the bottom of his robe where it was wet. The man felt great pity for the dog.

'This poor animal is thirsty, just as I was thirsty until I found this well', he said. 'He will die of thirst if he does not get water.'

The man stroked the dog's head. The dog wagged his tail. He was grateful for the water he had licked from the man's wet robe.

'Wait here,' the man said. 'I will get you some water.'

The man put first one leg, then the other leg over the side of the well, and began to climb downwards once more. Because he was no longer thirsty, he found the climb much easier than before.

When the man reached the water, he held onto the side of the well very tightly. Then, he took off his leather socks. He dipped the socks into the water until they were full. Then, he put the edges of the socks into his mouth and held them very firmly between his teeth.

He began to climb up the well again. But it was very hard this time. The socks full of water were very heavy, and his mouth and teeth began to hurt. But the man did not stop. Slowly, he climbed until he reached the top of the well.

When he reached the ground again, he knelt down and opened the first sock so that the dog could easily get his muzzle inside. The dog drank all the water without stopping. Then, the man opened the second sock, and he drank all the water in that sock, too.

All the time he was drinking, the dog's tail was wagging. The man smiled. 'This dog is happy now,' he said. 'He will not die of thirst and neither will I!'

Allah was very pleased with the man who had treated the thirsty dog so kindly. For this kind act, Allah forgave the man the sins he had committed in his life.

Here, the Blessed Prophet came to the end of the story. After he had finished speaking, one of his Companions said:

'O Messenger of Allah! If we are good to animals, will we also be forgiven our sins?'

'Yes,' the Blessed Prophet replied. 'You will be rewarded for being good to all living creatures.'

The man in the story went to paradise for his kind act.

3·the cruel woman and her cat

There was once a woman who had a cat. She was a cruel woman and treated her cat badly.

One day, the Blessed Prophet told his Companions a story about this bad woman.

'She did not look after the cat properly', he said.

'She did not give it anything to eat or drink.'

Because of this, the cat became very thin, and its fur began to fall out. The woman had a very bad temper. When she was angry, she used to kick her cat or throw it out through the door and make it stay out in the street all night.

Before long, the cat became very frightened of the woman. Each time she came near it, the cat cried and hid underneath a table or a chair.

The woman's neighbours were very angry with her. One day, a neighbour came to see her.

'You are very cruel to your cat!' the neighbour said.

'A cat is one of Allah's living creatures, just as we are! You are doing a great wrong!'

The woman was very angry when she heard this.

'Go away!' she shouted at her neighbour. 'The cat belongs to me. I will treat it badly if I want to! Go away and leave me alone!'

The neighbour was very unhappy to hear this. Then, he thought of a plan to save the cat. He went back to his house and waited until nightfall. Next door, he heard the cruel woman shouting at her cat.

'Get out of here, you dirty animal!' she shouted. 'I will not have you in my house tonight!'

The neighbour heard the cruel woman open her front door. Then, he heard the cat crying and howling as the woman threw it out into the street. Then, she slammed her door shut.

The neighbour waited for a few moments to make sure the woman would not come out of her house again. Then, he went out into the street. There was the cat, sitting pitifully by the woman's front door. The cat was crying and sniffing at the door, hoping the woman would open it and let it in.

The neighbour's heart was filled with pity for the cat.

'You poor creature', he said. 'Look how thin you are!' He bent down and picked up the cat. He stroked its head until it stopped crying.

'I will take you to my house', the neighbour said, 'and give you some food.'

When he got back to his house, he filled a plate with some food and gave it to the cat. The cat ate hungrily. Soon, the plate was empty. The neighbour filled the plate again. Again, it ate all the food very quickly. But at last, the cat had had enough food and lay down on the floor and fell fast asleep.

Next morning, the cruel woman could not find her cat. She looked everywhere. She searched in the street. She searched in the market. But the cat was nowhere to be found. The woman was very angry.

Someone has stolen my cat, she said to herself. Then, she remembered what her neighbour had said the previous day. He had tried to stop her treating her cat cruelly.

'That neighbour of mine has my cat!' she said. 'He must be the one who has stolen it!'

So, she went to her neighbour's house. She banged on the door and shouted angrily. The neighbour opened the door.

'I know you have stolen my cat!' the woman shouted at him. 'You are a thief! Give it back to me at once!'

'No', said the neighbour. 'You are a cruel woman and you do not deserve to have a cat!'

'I want that cat! Give it back', the woman shouted. She was getting angrier and angrier.

'I will not give you your cat until you promise that you will treat it kindly', the neighbour replied.

When the woman heard that, she laughed to herself.

Silly man! she thought. All I have to do is promise to treat my cat well, and he will give it back to me!

So, the woman pretended not to be angry any more. She smiled at her neighbour.

'Of course I will treat the cat well if you give it back to me!' she said in a friendly voice.

'You promise?' the neighbour demanded.

'Yes, yes, I promise,' the woman replied.

'You will give the cat enough to eat and you will not throw it out of the house at night?' the neighbour wanted to know.

'Of course not,' the woman said sweetly. 'I will feed the cat and look after it properly from now on. I will not be cruel to my cat ever again!'

Did the woman keep her promise? No, she did not. Unfortunately, though, the neighbour had believed her. He had not thought that she was telling lies. He gave the cat back to her.

The cruel woman took the cat back to her house and treated it more cruelly than ever before. She tied a rope round its neck and then tied the rope to a chair.

Once again, she gave the poor cat nothing to eat or drink. It became thinner and thinner and weaker and weaker. After a short while, it died.

'What a terrible thing to do!' cried one of the Companions of the Blessed Prophet. 'What a very cruel and wicked woman!'

The Blessed Prophet agreed. 'This made Allah very angry with the cruel woman', he told his Companions.

Of course the woman was not only cruel. She had told lies as well. She had committed a great sin because she had ill-treated one of Allah's living creatures.

The man who gave the thirsty dog water was forgiven his sins because he acted kindly towards a living creature. But this woman who treated her cat cruelly was not forgiven her sins, so Allah sent her to Hell.

4 • the crying camel

The city of Madina, where the Blessed Prophet lived, was a beautiful city. There were many gardens around the city. In the gardens, there were many trees. When the sun shone brightly during the daytime, the trees gave cool shade. The Muslims who lived in Madina used to sit in the shade to get out of the hot, burning sun.

One day, the Blessed Prophet went for a walk through Madina to meet with the Muslims and talk to them. After a while, he came to a garden and went in.

There was a man sitting under a tree, in the cool shade. There were many other Muslims in the garden, too. Then, the Blessed Prophet saw a camel standing in one corner of the garden. The camel was tied to a post. It was making a pitiful howling sound.

The Blessed Prophet walked over to where the camel was tied up. As he got closer, he saw that the camel was crying. Big tears were rolling down its cheeks and making the fur on its face all wet.

The Blessed Prophet felt great pity for the camel. He went up to it and stroked its fur, and wiped away its tears. The Blessed Prophet saw that the camel was very thin. After a while, the camel stopped crying and howling. It gave a snort, as camels do when they are pleased.

The Blessed Prophet looked around at all the people standing in the garden.

'Who is the owner of this camel?' he asked. The man who had been sitting beneath the tree stepped forward.

'I am the owner of the camel, O Messenger of God!' he said.

The Blessed Prophet told him that he had been very cruel to the camel. The poor animal was howling and crying because his owner made it work very hard, but did not give it enough to eat and drink. Everyone in the garden could see how thin the camel was and how cruelly the man had acted towards the camel. When the owner of the camel heard this, he began to feel ashamed.

'Do you not fear Allah because of this camel?' the Blessed Prophet asked him. Allah had given the camel into the man's care to help him in his work and carry burdens for him. The man had a duty to treat the camel well and see that it had enough to eat and drink. If he did so, the camel would work well for him.

The owner of the camel now felt very ashamed indeed.

'I have done wrong!' he said. 'The camel is one of Allah's living creatures. I am sorry for my cruelty.'

All living creatures must be treated kindly. The Blessed Prophet always taught that if they were treated well, Allah would be pleased. But if they were treated badly, Allah would be angry.

The camel owner never forgot what the Blessed Prophet told him. After this, he always looked after his camels properly. Although the camels still worked hard, for they were strong animals, the man always saw that they had enough food and water.

5·a sparrow and her young ones

One day, the Blessed Prophet Muhammad was travelling with some Companions. After they had gone some way, they decided to stop and rest.

The Blessed Prophet left his Companions for a short time and while he was away, they amused themselves watching the birds flying around in the sky. There were many different sorts of birds. Then, one of the Blessed Prophet's Companions pointed upwards.

'Look!' he said to the others. 'There is a pretty bird. It looks like a mother bird because there are two young birds with her! The two young birds must be her fledglings!'

The bird was a sparrow and the two small birds were indeed her fledglings. The three birds flew round and round above the men's heads. They watched them with pleasure because the birds were very beautiful. But the young fledglings were not so good at flying as their mother was. Gradually, as they flew above the heads of the men, they began to get lower and lower.

'Let us catch them!' one of the men cried. 'It will be so easy!'

The others agreed with him, and after a while, the little fledglings came low enough for them to put up their hands and catch them. When the fledglings felt the hands close around them, they struggled and shrieked in fright. But the men were too strong for them and however hard they struggled, they could not escape.

At last, the little birds were exhausted and lay still. The Blessed Prophet's Companions came to look at them, they stroked the birds' feathers with their fingers.

They were very gentle with the birds, because the Blessed Prophet had always told them that they must treat living creatures kindly and gently. They did not mean to harm the birds. They just wanted to have a close look at them.

But the mother bird, flying round and round high above their heads, did not know this. She thought the men meant to kill her babies, or at least keep them as captives. So, she cried and shrieked and kept on swooping down near the men, trying to make them let go of her two little birds.

The men waved their arms to keep her away, and before long, the mother bird was very distressed. She cried and shrieked more loudly than ever.

Suddenly, while all this was going on, the Blessed Prophet returned. He saw the mother bird flying round and round and heard her crying. At once, he realized she was very unhappy and when he saw his Companions holding the little birds he knew what had caused her unhappiness.

'Who has caused trouble to this sparrow by taking away her young ones?' the Blessed Prophet asked.

The little birds must be released, he told his Companions. They should be allowed to join their mother, who was frightened for their safety.

The Blessed Prophet's Companions obeyed him at once. They opened their hands. The little birds struggled for a while, and then spread their wings and flew upwards. They reached their mother high up in the sky, and together, the three birds flew away and out of sight.

It was a happy thing to see. The mother bird was no longer distressed and the fledglings were no longer frightened. Because the three birds were happy, the hearts of the Blessed Prophet's Companions were happy, too.

The Blessed Prophet was content. He had been un-happy to see the mother bird in trouble. But now, all was well again.